Acting Edition

Wet Brain

by John J. Caswell, Jr.

ISBN 978-0-573-71101-5

www.concordtheatricals.com
www.concordtheatricals.co.uk

FOR PRODUCTION INQUIRIES

UNITED STATES AND CANADA
info@concordtheatricals.com
1-866-979-0447

UNITED KINGDOM AND EUROPE
licensing@concordtheatricals.co.uk
020-7054-7298

Each title is subject to availability from Concord Theatricals Corp.,
depending upon country of performance. Please be aware that *WET
BRAIN* may not be licensed by Concord Theatricals Corp. in your
territory. Professional and amateur producers should contact the
nearest Concord Theatricals Corp. office or licensing partner to verify
availability.

WET BRAIN was first produced by Playwrights Horizons (Adam Greenfield, Artistic Director; Leslie Marcus, Managing Director) and MCC Theater (Bernie Telsey & Will Cantler, Artistic Directors; Blake West, Executive Director) in New York City on May 19, 2023. The production was supported in part by the National Endowment for the Arts. It was directed by Dustin Wills, with scenic design by Kate Noll, costume design by Haydee Zelideth Antuñano, lighting design by Cha See, sound design by Tei Blow and John Gasper, projection design by Nick Hussong, prop design by Matt Carlin, and fight choreography by J. David Brimmer. The Production Stage Manager was Kasson Marroquin and the Assistant Stage Manager was Kelsey Vivian. The cast was as follows:

RON	Frankie J. Alvarez
ANGELINA	Ceci Fernández
MONA	Florencia Lozano
JOE	Julio Monge
RICKY	Arturo Luíz Soria

In 2021, *WET BRAIN* received the L. Arnold Weissberger Award for Playwriting, jointly administered by the Anna L. Weissberger Foundation and Williamstown Theatre Festival.

CHARACTERS

JOE – Mid-to-late sixties. Father. First-generation Mexican American. Mechanic. End-stage alcoholic. Widower.

RICKY – Early forties. Joe's son returned home from New York City. Gay.

RON – Late forties. Joe's son. Lives locally and works with his father.

ANGELINA – Mid-to-late thirties. Joe's daughter. Has never left home. Nursing school student.

MONA – Mid-to-late sixties were she still alive. Joe's deceased wife and mother of his kids.

CRYSTAL – Mid-to-late sixties. A home-health aide. Friend of Angelina.

RECORDED VOICES – Including **RECORDING**, **OPERATOR**, and the **TV HOST**.

MONA, **CRYSTAL**, and **RECORDED VOICES** should be played by one actor, in support of a cross-dimensional presence of **MONA**.

Do not list **CRYSTAL** or **RECORDED VOICES** in the program or any other publicity materials. The actor should only be credited in advance as playing **MONA**.

SETTING

Scottsdale, Arizona.
And outer space.

TIME

Summer.

AUTHOR'S NOTES

Necessary scenic elements

A kitchen window over a sink with a passable area beyond it, the outdoors visible to the audience. Here, Joe will place a ladder on which we see him ascend (or indicate ascension) to the roof.

A playable roof that should feel dangerously high even if it isn't.

Multiple dark hallways leading to the primary playing space that is at the center of the house. These hallways lead to the unseen locations of Joe's bedroom, Angelina's bedroom, a bathroom, a family room, and perhaps other unnamed spaces of your own imagining.

An unseen front door down a dark hallway. When opened, the door beeps three times from an old security system. The beeps precede an actor's entrance by several seconds as they must travel the hallway to arrive at the center of the house, our playing area.

A looming and large carob tree that becomes more prominent during the roof scene.

A distorted version of the family's family room, recreated inside of a spacecraft operated by Joe in zero gravity. It is also the inside of his deteriorating mind. Executing this should not necessarily require expensive effects or machinery. Consider simple theater magic and sparse but affecting gesture rather than complex mechanical sets. In a black box, for example, the walls of the theatre might serve as additional playing surfaces. You might utilize ladders to achieve height. Or wheeled scaffolding to move people through simulated space travel. You might have actors or crew manipulate objects by hand, such as a lamp floating across the room. The space scene is a call to creativity, point-of-view, and resourcefulness. It's not an expectation of costly technical wizardry.

Style notes

A sentence with little punctuation or heavy use of comma indicates an invitation toward a scattered rambling that is a mode of communication often used by this family.

A / indicates overlap and the location where the following character's dialogue should begin.

A [ ] briefly interrupts actor dialogue and only occurs in Act Three, Scene One. It represents a sudden split-second blip in visuals and sound, as if the signal of reality is cutting in and out, digitally.

For my father, if he's still out there.
For my sister and my brother.

ACT ONE

One

(Clouds obscure a bright summer moon, casting a shadow over a shitty neighborhood sidewalk somewhere in Scottsdale, AZ.)

(The whispered groan of a hot and humid breeze. Then a swelling chorus of cicadas join the rustling leaves of a carob tree.)

(JOE appears from shadow dressed in shorts and a shirt nearly translucent from wear. His flip-flops incoherently flip and flop. He carries a bag of water bottles and drinks from one already open. Then, in a small and strangled voice –)

JOE.
SHA-SHA, FOO-FOO, POO-SHA-POON
LOTTABABY-IN-A-BASSEN-LIKEUH-SHERMA-SAZOON
I SAIDUH SAH-SAH BOOM-BOOM –

(An unlit streetlamp begins to flash above him, interrupting his song. He watches mesmerized until the lamp finds electric purchase, snapping itself on steadily. He points at the light –)

Wha' you sayin' me?

(The streetlamp's glow intensifies along with the sound of surging power. Louder and brighter as **JOE** *is drawn toward its increasingly alien yellow light, reaching toward it, rising to his toes as he says –)*

JOE.

SHA-SAH. SAAAH.

HEY!! AAAAAAAAAAAAH!

(And just as he seems ready to leave the Earth entirely, a car horn from behind a pair of headlights. The streetlight snaps to normal, reality restoring. A car door opens, footsteps, then –)

RICKY. *(Voice-over.)* Dad?

Two

(A filthy kitchen under remodel connecting openly to a dining room whose dining table has long been replaced by a decrepit recliner, a crunchy futon, an outdated television, and stacks of tile, tools, and other general evidence of renovations derailed.)

(Plastic water bottles are scattered around, all of the same name brand.)

(Several dark hallways loom like fat-clogged arteries leading to other parts of the house.)

(A sliding glass door leads to a backyard that is almost entirely a swimming pool.)

*(****ANGELINA*** *on the futon studying a nursing textbook, headphones around her neck.* **RICKY***, his suitcase nearby, opens the refrigerator, the light inside flickering on his horrified face.)*

RICKY. Oh my God, it's alive!

ANGELINA. Close that, stop looking inside of shit!

RICKY. Pick up a sponge once in a while, Angelina.

ANGELINA. Yeah then go sleep at the shop / if you don't like it!

RICKY. It smells like shit in here! You got intelligent life living up in your fucking freezer!

ANGELINA. It's not my fucking freezer, I need QUIET.

RICKY. No you need soap, I'll make a list, and food! I'm fucking starving, you got nothing, hey how old is this mail, what is this, *Desert Botanical Garden: Dear Joseph, We hope you never leaf us, we're very frond of your donation as it means healthy plants and well-maintained* – who's writing his checks? You or Ron?

*(**RICKY** flips a switch and an ugly fluorescent flickers on with great effort.)*

ANGELINA. No big light, I'll get a migraine!

RICKY. On another fucking planet, where are you?

ANGELINA. No where the fuck are *you*? Six fucking years, Ricky.

RICKY. More like four.

ANGELINA. After the second DUI.

RICKY. Yeah okay fine, six years if you say so.

ANGELINA. No it's not about me saying so, it's six six six.

RICKY. So then why aren't you happy to see me?

ANGELINA. It's just a fucking Thursday night over here, I said hello.

RICKY. Yeah but what's going on?

ANGELINA. He can't talk anymore, I send you all those fucking emails!

RICKY. Okay what happened is that I'm not really good with emails at the moment.

ANGELINA. What the hell does that mean, at the moment not / good with emails?

RICKY. ADHD I guess, I'm overwhelmed, I'm fine. / Hey what is that, what are you reading?

ANGELINA. You never come home, you don't do the phone, you don't text back, so I send you emails! That was *your* fucking idea, Ricky! / And hardly ever!

RICKY. There's nothing I can do from eight hours away!

ANGELINA. Five-and-a-half hours nonstop. / I checked, you lied.

RICKY. No you have to include to-and-from-airport travel time.

ANGELINA. It's become very clear, Ricky is off the map.

RICKY. I am not off, look at me, do I look off the map? / Nevermind!

ANGELINA. I'd have to see you in daylight, your skin.

RICKY. *(Holding up the donor letter.)* He doesn't even like plants, he falls on top of plants.

ANGELINA. I'm not talking about the mail with you right now.

RICKY. *Corporate Donor, Copper Circle.* The shop can't afford this.

ANGELINA. That's between you and Ron, I am not the shop.

RICKY. *Cordially invited to the Under the Stars Gala,* open bar, / can you imagine?

ANGELINA. It's a mistake or something, are you gonna talk to Ron or not?!

RICKY. What the fuck do I need talk to Ron about?!

ANGELINA. I'm out on the first, I signed a lease. / You saw that email, you're here.

RICKY. Yeah I saw that particular email, I am *not* here!

ANGELINA. Four times in like fifteen years.

RICKY. It's Arizona, what the fuck am I coming back here for?

ANGELINA. Historically to hide out or dry out, not for us.

RICKY. You signed a lease, what am I supposed to do? I can't fly across the country every time his organs start to shut down.

ANGELINA. You could've at least come for the kidney.

RICKY. They knew what I thought about that. / I was working eighty-plus!

ANGELINA. Yeah and I told Ron not to do it, too, that's not the point, yeah you have a really good job, God knows why, / you're not exactly dependable.

RICKY. It's called an MBA, go get your own.

ANGELINA. You barely got through that program. So who'd you fuck at the career fair?

RICKY. Hey, are you hungry? My treat.

ANGELINA. No I'm not hungry you jerk, I feel like shit, I'm probably dying.

RICKY. I'm probably dead.

ANGELINA. I can't fucking breathe anymore, I keep clenching my jaw.

RICKY. It's called stress, you gotta learn to live with it.

ANGELINA. You better shut the fuck up talking to me about stress.

RICKY. Four words for you: Alternate. Nostril. / Breathing. Exercises.

ANGELINA. I'm serious Ricky, no listen to me, sometimes my heart stops.

RICKY. You mean like poetically, me too.

ANGELINA. No it's called stress-induced arrhythmia.

RICKY. See? Stress!

ANGELINA. Heart-stopping stress!

RICKY. Speaking of clogged arteries.

> (**RICKY** *holds up suddenly-found pizza coupons.*)

ANGELINA. No fucking way.

RICKY. What do you think? We get three large?

ANGELINA. Why would you get three large pizzas?!

RICKY. Add twenty-four wings for only $12.99?

ANGELINA. That's like twelve dead chickens.

RICKY. No there's two eating wings in every one flying wing so it's six.

ANGELINA. We can't eat pizza together, Rick. We get sick.

RICKY. We can freeze some for leftovers.

ANGELINA. We don't have leftovers when we do this, / we eat the fucking boxes.

RICKY. We'll set out two pieces each, wrap the rest in foil, / mummify that shit.

ANGELINA. No not for me, not even two pieces, I'm rewiring my mind.

RICKY. You're wasting away!

ANGELINA. Don't talk about my fucking body! It's not about weight.

RICKY. Normal people do cocaine and call it a day.

ANGELINA. Are you doing cocaine?!

RICKY. No come on I'm fat one minute then I'm skinny the next, / it's normal for me.

ANGELINA. That's not normal, you got that little Buddha-belly for life now.

RICKY. Jesus Christ, fine, we'll order the chopped salads.

ANGELINA. Those salads are mostly croutons, you might as well eat pizza.

RICKY. I can put in the special comments *don't put the croutons.*

ANGELINA. They put more that way.

RICKY. You restrict yourself too much, something gives. / It can't be food.

ANGELINA. I have to do both at one time, they feed off each other.

RICKY. You go too far.

ANGELINA. You should go further. Visceral fat literally strangles your liver.

RICKY. Visceral fat, how fucking dare you.

> (*A crash from outside.* **RICKY** *looks out the kitchen window.*)

ANGELINA. Was that Dad?

RICKY. He's under the tree, we have to get him inside.

ANGELINA. He's not going anywhere, he got what he wanted.

RICKY. I guess the court can't take away his legs.

ANGELINA. File the motion, let's see what they say.

> (**RICKY** *finds a cigarette case on the counter.*
> **ANGELINA** *rushes to get it from him. The*
> *following happens over a physical struggle*
> *for the case.*)

Ricky, give it to me.

RICKY. Is this Mom's cigarette case?

ANGELINA. Well she's dead, she doesn't possess, so no.

RICKY. Are you smoking again?

ANGELINA. I use it for quarters! The washer's broken by the way.

RICKY. Where'd you get it from?!

ANGELINA. I don't know, it was around!

RICKY. It's been thirty years, throw her shit out!

> (*The struggle ends in* **ANGELINA** *taking the*
> *case forcefully from* **RICKY** *and knocking*

over a bottle of Joe's pills. **RICKY** *kneels to collect the pills.* **ANGELINA** *doesn't help him.)*

Does he take all of these pills when he's supposed to?

ANGELINA. I put them out on the counter in the morning.

RICKY. You should be watching him swallow.

ANGELINA. You can watch him swallow all you want, welcome to heaven.

RICKY. I'm not staying.

ANGELINA. He can't live here alone, / set him up somewhere.

RICKY. I don't know about that yet. I'm gonna watch, we're gonna see.

ANGELINA. No *you're* gonna see! I've seen, he needs a home.

RICKY. Do you know how much that costs?

ANGELINA. You swim in coin like *DuckTales*, I've seen pics of your apartment.

RICKY. I'm not doing shit for him, I can't fucking stand that man.

ANGELINA. Oh, please. Dad called *everybody* a faggot back then, it was his catch-all.

RICKY. I don't care what happens to him, Angie.

ANGELINA. He's a bag of meat with rights, you gotta throw some money at this.

RICKY. I paid for his last one. Look I know you think I can drop everything but –

ANGELINA. Literally nobody thinks that. I didn't even message Ron, I'm waiting to see if you stay longer than ten minutes before you put the whole country between us again.

RICKY. I was lucky I got out of here alive.

ANGELINA. Yeah and I still haven't!

> (*Three beeps indicating the entrance of a person through the carport door, offstage, down a hall.*)

Listen, you wanna keep five feet away in case he pukes. And don't make eye contact.

RICKY. I can't handle this shit, I can stay at the Sheraton.

ANGELINA. Is that all you got in you? Twenty minutes?

> (**JOE** *grunts from darkness, unseen, silencing them. Then he slowly emerges with his bag of water bottles.*)

RICKY. Dad?

> (**RICKY** *turns on the hall light.* **JOE** *is startled by it and shouts aggressively and incomprehensibly at* **RICKY** *in reaction.* **ANGELINA** *overtakes* **JOE** *in voice, yelling, snapping her fingers until he is calm again.*)

What the fuck are you doing?!

ANGELINA. You have to make yourself bigger than he is.

> (**JOE** *kicks a water bottle in* **RICKY**'s *direction.*)

RICKY. What's with all the water bottles?

ANGELINA. He buys the vodka, he buys the water, he goes into the grocery store bathroom, dumps out the water, pours in the vodka, brings it home. He's hiding it from me.

> (*A liquid spills from* **JOE**'s *mouth, down the front of his shirt.*)

Yep there she is, Old Faithful. What did I say? He's a fucking garbage can.

RICKY. It's not his fault.

ANGELINA. He's a dirty fucking pig.

RICKY. He can hear what you're saying!

ANGELINA. He's not listening. Watch. Dad! Say hi to Ricky! Ricky, talk.

RICKY. Hey Dad. We're gonna get this tile laid once and for all, right?

ANGELINA. You don't have to do your bro voice anymore.

RICKY. I don't do a fucking bro voice, Angelina!

ANGELINA. Dad, Ricky's gonna get you set up once I'm gone.

RICKY. No, I'm gonna get you caught up on a few things and then I gotta get back to work because I'm not responsible for anyone but myself.

ANGELINA. I'm not fucking around about the first.

RICKY. Hey, you hear that, Dad? She can't take it anymore. You gotta focus on your health. Hey, you hearing me? What the fuck is he looking at?

> *(Reality snaps instantly to a liminal space,* **JOE***, isolated from the others despite their physical presence. A version of the three beeps that is stranger than the original. A dark figure in the hallway, shrouded, oozing threads of ink that spread like veins.)*

ANGELINA. *(Affected, underwater, muffled.)* He sees shit we can't see. He's turning into someone else, look at his eyes.

> *(The room snaps back to normal for a very brief moment, both sound and visuals disappearing long enough for –)*

(Clearly now.) He sees shit we can't see. He's turning into someone else, look at his eyes.

(*The room snaps back to* **JOE***'s chaotic perspective. He opens the fridge, a rush of ghost cicadas flying toward him, causing him to stumble.*)

(**RICKY** *closes the refrigerator door, restoring objective reality instantly, cicadas vanishing.* **JOE** *falls to the ground.*)

RICKY. Shit he went down hard.

ANGELINA. No he's fine, leave him where he's at.

RICKY. Should I kick him in the ribs while I'm at it?

ANGELINA. You put him back on his feet and he falls over somewhere else.

RICKY. He's bleeding, Angelina!

ANGELINA. That's dried up from yesterday.

RICKY. Why what happened yesterday?!

ANGELINA. That did!

RICKY. Help me lift him up!

ANGELINA. I'm not pulling out my back, I start practicals tomorrow. Cover him with a blanket, lock yourself in the empty bedroom if you actually wanna sleep, otherwise you got the crusty futon.

(**RICKY** *tends to* **JOE** *as* **ANGELINA** *starts to leave –*)

RICKY. Hey. I'm having that dream again.

(*– then she stops for a moment.*)

ANGELINA. Ricky, I am so fucking tired.

(**ANGELINA** *leaves down a hall, slams her bedroom door, lights out.*)

Three

(Friday morning, 2 AM.)

*(The very old TV snaps on, **RICKY** asleep in its glow. A soft hammering from deep in the house. It stops. Some time.)*

*(**JOE** shuffles into the kitchen from darkness wearing a ski mask and an old fur coat. He carries a hammer. He stands in front of **RICKY** for a moment, then reaches toward the ceiling. A light fixture begins to glow yellow.)*

*(**RICKY** turns over in his sleep and the light immediately snaps to normal at the disturbance, piercing a hole in what was **JOE**'s encroaching perspective. **RICKY** wakes with **JOE** standing over him.)*

RICKY. Whoa, Jesus! Dad? Hey, what are you doing, are you alright?

> *(**JOE** moves to a corner. Prepares himself. Pisses on the ground.)*

Angelina?!

> *(No one comes. Once the pissing ends, ski-masked **JOE** shuffles to the recliner and sits down, staring at the TV.)*

> *(Intrigued by **JOE**'s deterioration, **RICKY** pulls out his phone and puts **JOE** on camera, then snaps a picture of him using both flash and sound.)*

> *(A dark, quiet moment as **JOE** pulls off his ski mask.)*

> *(**RICKY** then takes another photo, the flash followed by complete darkness.)*

Four

(8 AM, Friday morning.)

(A few stealthy beams of sunlight smuggle themselves through layers of iron bars and thick window coverings. The sound of a crow cawing outside. **RICKY** *asleep on the futon, mouth hanging wide open.)*

(Three beeps.)

RON. *(Off, from down the hallway.)* Yo Dad I could really use your fucking help today. Three paint jobs behind and ugly Aunt Cathy wants her oil changed so get your ass up!

*(***RON*** *enters wearing a navy blue polo tucked into jeans, belted mid-butt-cheek. He carries a bag of several breakfast burritos.)*

(The sound of someone splashing, swimming in the pool outside.)

*(***RON*** *sees* ***RICKY***, *then takes a foil-covered burrito from the bag and holds it near his own crotch, making a burrito penis. He then inserts the edge of the burrito penis into* ***RICKY****'s mouth, seeing how much he can manage to fit inside.* ***RICKY*** *wakes with a gag and a shout.)*

Rise and shine, cocksucker!

RICKY. Ow fuck, Ron! It's burning, it has aluminum foil!

*(***RON*** *smacks* ***RICKY***, ***RICKY*** *immediately smacks back a little harder,* ***RON*** *smacks again, but much harder.)*

My God that hurt my brain you stupid little bitch!

RON. Goddamn dude you sound like way more homosexual.

RICKY. You're a fucking cave person.

RON. I'm a cave *man*, I'm not a fucking person! Why you so serious, girl?

RICKY. Uh, fucked in the face by a burrito!

RON. See you sound way more fagged-out on the word *burrito*.

RICKY. Curse of the cocksucker. You get loosey-lips, you develop our dialect.

RON. Yeah you even sleep gay now, you're all ready for it and shit.

RICKY. What can I say bro, I'm a dirty fucking hole open twenty-four seven.

> (**RON** *punches* **RICKY** *in the arm,* **RICKY** *folds over in pain.*)

Ow my God, you're primitive, you never change.

RON. I was homophobic way before you turned gay and *I'm* supposed to change?

RICKY. No of course not.

RON. Irregardless, just so we're clear on something, Ricky. You better not be keeping any fucking thing of yours open twenty-four seven, you hear me right now? Be safe, have some fucking self-respect!

RICKY. Wow that's actually very sweet of you, Ron.

> (**RON** *aggressively throws a burrito at* **RICKY**.)

RON. Eat up, I like you better when you're fat.

RICKY. What is it, egg and chorizo?

RON. It's fucking breakfast time, isn't it?

RICKY. You get it from Fiesta?

RON. Uh yeah where the fuck else dude?

RICKY. Filibertos?

RON. No don't ever go there, it's dog meat.

RICKY. No that's like an urban legend.

RON. Yeah but there has to be a reason why.

> (*A splash from the pool outside surprises*
> **RICKY**.)

RICKY. Is that Angelina?

RON. Yeah she's out there spouting.

RICKY. Wow so she started swimming again?

RON. Every morning, back and forth, inhaling all that krill.

RICKY. Don't say shit like that, she's being weird about pizza.

RON. The two of you were an eating machine, it was fucking binge-cest.

RICKY. Well thanks for being so, hey you know about eating disorders, right?

RON. Yeah totally, it's called –

> (**RON** *makes a brief pig snort. Beat.* **JOE**
> *retches from offstage.*)

Dad come have breakfast so you can throw up better!

RICKY. Is he okay in there?

RON. He's fine, he's the ideal male specimen in the prime of his life, like you fucking care.

RICKY. What about you? I mean you were ripped last time, now you're like, / are you eating enough?

RON. It's under control, change the fucking subject!

RICKY. Are you still over on Roosevelt, with uh.

RON. Eva, you stupid! / Fifteen years me and her but whatever.

RICKY. Eva shit sorry, I can't remember anything anymore.

RON. Hey, I'm just here to pick up Dad.

RICKY. For what? He can't work, not like that.

RON. As long as he puts on the uniform, I swing by.

RICKY. It's a little weird.

RON. He eats, he drinks, he passes out, I leave. Same thing tomorrow.

RICKY. It's a waste of gas.

RON. Yo I'm driving a cute little Nissan Leaf these days, don't worry.

RICKY. Are you serious?

RON. Gay dude! Of course not, same F150, Ford for life! Hey, I've been coming since they took his license. It used to be we'd get coffee, do the ten hours, close up the shop, then go visit the titties over at Dream Palace.

RICKY. Gross.

RON. Sometimes. Then he started getting sick around lunchtime so I'd bring him home early. Kept getting earlier. Now we do this. We get shit up and running, that's the part he's still good at. The shop dude, that's something else.

RICKY. I don't wanna talk about the shop.

RON. There's no fucking cash, I fucked up the books. Connie don't come, we can't pay.

RICKY. I'm not walking outta there again with a broken jaw.

RON. Nobody's gonna gay bash you at the shop anymore, Ricky. Except for me.

RICKY. I don't want anything to do with that fucking auto body shop, Ron!

RON. You don't want anything to do with anything, I'm doing everything I can here, you know that? Look! At least he gets himself cleaned up in the morning, right? I do that. Me. What the fuck are you looking at?!

RICKY. Are you sick? You're so tiny, you look really creepy.

(**RON** *grabs* **RICKY** *by the shirt, near the neck.*)

RON. Hey where the fuck have you been, piece of shit?! Mr. Fucking CFO?!

RICKY. VP of Finance but thanks for the promotion, let go of me, skeleton freak!

(*The sliding glass door opens,* **ANGELINA** *in a robe. She's back and forth to and from the bedroom until she leaves.*)

ANGELINA. Hey, manchild!! Get your hands off him!!

(**RON** *releases* **RICKY.**)

RON. Good morning to you too, *Shamu!*

RICKY. I told him to quit with the whale shit.

ANGELINA. Don't worry, I feel nothing, it's every single day.

RON. Actually you're more like a dolphin these days.

ANGELINA. Yeah at least I don't buy my pants in little boy husky.

RON. That was a compliment, the dolphin thing!

ANGELINA. You're giving me a ride today, Crystal's sick.

RON. Fine but I can't wait for your hair to dry, we fired Alejandro.

RICKY. Who's Crystal?

RON. / Alejandro's toast, three kids but whatever.

ANGELINA. Crystal is, who cares Ron, oh sad sorry, Crystal's my teacher, she's a nurse, she's a mindreader. Rick, her ex-husband is gay.

RON. Angie has the hots for this chick, it's not good.

ANGELINA. I emailed you, she does in-house.

RICKY. Nursing or mind reading?

ANGELINA. Ricky says he's not good with emails.

RICKY. At the moment.

RON. Oh shit, are you off the map, Ricky?

RICKY. Stop fucking saying that!

RON. No, come on. How's our little pact going, huh?! Should we do a check-in?

ANGELINA. You better fucking cool it, Ron, you're turning red.

RICKY. Nurse, mindreader, teacher, what kind of school are you going to?

RON. SCC, she's gonna be an RN.

ANGELINA. CNA.

RON. Just say registered nurse, it sounds better.

ANGELINA. Is that okay, Rick? Am I allowed an education by near middle-age?

RICKY. Yeah but why can't you keep living here for that.

ANGELINA. Ron you said you'd talk to him!

RON. No you said you'd tell him to talk to *me*!

RICKY. What do you wanna talk me about, Ron?

RON. I have no idea, ask Angelina! Hey, you know what? We should get up on the roof.

ANGELINA. Oh my God, you and the goddamn roof!

RICKY. I'm not going up on the fucking roof, especially not with you.

RON. I gotta check it out, Angie heard something moving around up there.

ANGELINA. A really long time ago, why do you keep saying that?! Ron, talk to him.

> (**ANGELINA** *dips out.*)

RON. She's serious man, she's outta here.

RICKY. Yeah okay and then what?

RON. You tell me, aren't you from corporate or something?

RICKY. Give me a minute, part of me is still, I'm not here.

> (**RON** *throws a balled up foil wrapper, hits* **RICKY**'s *head.*)

RON. You're here. And she's exhausted, man.

RICKY. Are you doing everything you can to help her out?

RON. What the fuck you say to me?!

RICKY. That was an error. I take it back.

RON. You go in there, rip out the fucking kidney he promised not to shit all over, then maybe we talk about me upping my game.

RICKY. Sorry.

RON. Jesus.

RICKY. So. Okay come over here after work. Bring whatever bank stuff you can find. I can get something for the grill.

RON. Maybe, yeah. Because I gotta get up on the roof anyway, check it out.

(**ANGELINA** *enters wearing scrubs, hair back,
still wet.*)

RICKY. What's wrong with the roof exactly, what are we
checking?

ANGELINA. Just some kids get up there sometimes, they
like climbing the tree.

RON. Yeah because it's a really good tree, that's why.

ANGELINA. I'll be home late, I'm getting dinner with Crystal.

RON. Fucking lesbians.

ANGELINA. She's my mentor Ron, she's like upper-fifties.

RICKY. Where's his insurance papers?

ANGELINA. Filing cabinet, top drawer. It lapsed a year ago.

RICKY. Where's the filing cabinet?

(**RON** *and* **ANGELINA** *conspire against* **RICKY**
in an instant.)

ANGELINA. In the family room.

RON. In the family room!

ANGELINA. In the family room!!!

RON. Look at his face, he's gonna shit his pants!

ANGELINA. He's having his little dreams again.

RICKY. What are you keeping shit in the family room for?

ANGELINA. What's wrong with the family room as a
storage solution, Rick?

RICKY. Nothing. Be careful though, he's pissing all over
the place.

ANGELINA. Oh shit, he pissed? Where, right there?

RICKY. Yeah, right there.

ANGELINA. Yeah that's his pissing corner.

RICKY. Are you fucking kidding me?

ANGELINA. I put a bucket there sometimes but he moves it, I can't stop him!

RON. We gotta rip this whole place apart one day, get down to the dirt.

ANGELINA. It's like in the foundation, it's pointless. Ron, let's go.

RICKY. Hey wait I wanted to show you something!

ANGELINA. Text me for emergencies only.

RICKY. I took this weird picture of Dad.

RON. Wow what a fucking creep, probably a nude.

ANGELINA. Look in the family room, whatever you need, it's all there.

> (**RON** *and* **ANGELINA** *are now out of sight.*)

> (*Three beeps.*)

RICKY. You know it's her birthday soon, right?

> (*A brief silence as the two unseen* **SIBLINGS** *process the idea of their dead mother being born. Then the door slams. Hard. Truck starts, then leaves.*)

> (**RICKY** *unwraps the burrito, stares blankly down a hall, eats in the slightly slovenly way you do when alone.* **JOE** *enters, shuffling silently toward* **RICKY**, *then standing very close, undetected.* **RICKY** *finally sees* **JOE** *and jumps.*)

I'm here. Now what the fuck do you want?

*(**JOE** slowly opens his mouth, at first looking as if he were trying to speak. Then he opens his mouth wider still, like a snake dislocating its jaw for a rat. **RICKY** brings the burrito closer to **JOE**'s mouth. Lights out just as **JOE** is about to take a bite.)*

Five

(The same day, evening.)

RECORDING. You have reached the customer support center for HEA Plus, Access, and the Department of Economic Security Family Assistance Administration. To continue in English, press one. Para continuar en Español, oprima el dos. For any other –

> *(A beep as "One" is pressed.)*

Please enter your date of birth by using month, date, then year, followed by the pound sign. For example, if your birthday is July 4, 1976, you would enter zero seven zero –

> *(Multi-toned beeps as the following sequence is pressed: zero six two three one nine five eight pound.)*

You entered June –

> *(A beep as "One" is pressed three times in a row, so angry.)*

Please hold for the next available representative.

> *(The disembodied call relocates to his cell's speakerphone, now playing instrumental bossa nova hold music.* He opens the fridge, grabs a plate of hamburgers and cheese. On the way back outside –)*

RICKY. Dad?

---

* A license to produce *Wet Brain* does not include a performance license for any third-party or copyrighted music. Licensees should create an original composition or use music in the public domain. For further information, please see the Music and Third-Party Materials Use Note on page iii.

JOE. *(From offstage.)* Grunt

RICKY. You okay in there?

>*(Nothing. **RICKY** sets his phone down, exits. The sound of sizzling meat. The hold music ends. **RICKY** reenters trying to pick up the phone but his hands are covered in ground beef.)*

Hello?

OPERATOR. Hello?

RICKY. Hello, I'm here.

OPERATOR. Sir, are you on a speakerphone?

RICKY. You sound kinda familiar.

OPERATOR. We've got a bad connection.

RICKY. No we don't, I'm picking up, wait.

>*(**RICKY** picks up the phone.)*

Hi. Hello. Yes. I love you. Thank God.

…

No, that's my father's birthday, but yeah, that's correct, uh-huh.

…

Yeah he had insurance but it dropped for nonpayment.

…

He's an alcoholic, he maxed out his substance abuse benefit.

…

They only cover two rehabs, I paid for the third and half.

…

RICKY. He's self-employed. Mechanic. Auto body. Family
business.

...

Okay great, can he file for disability at the same time?

...

Yeah. I can hold.

> (**RICKY** *exits to tend the grill, leaving his
> phone behind. The bossa nova hold music
> returns. A few moments pass, meat sizzling
> outside. Then suddenly –*)

> (**JOE** *falls down the stairs and crawls into
> the kitchen on all fours, clutching his side.
> He reaches the sink and pulls himself up. He
> removes his shirt and grabs a knife.*)

> (*He starts to cut into his side. The lamps
> flicker. Blood drips from the wound. He's
> searching for something.*)

> (**JOE** *digs his fingers into the wound and
> pulls out something round. It glows neon
> yellow. He holds it up to the ceiling.*)

> (*The room snaps to* **JOE**'s *perspective, chaos
> encroaching.*)

> (*Three beeps from front door, but they come
> through as distorted.*)

> (**ANGELINA** *appears from the hallway, just
> getting home.*)

ANGELINA. *(Distorted.)* Dad?!

> (*In an instant, we snap back to objective
> reality. The glowing yellow orb that Joe dug*

*from himself has vanished. The bossa nova
hold music plays on. He drops the knife.)*

Ricky!!

(**RICKY** *appears suddenly.)*

End Act One

ACT TWO

One

(Two weeks later. 10 PM, Friday night. Joe's house. Enough has changed to confirm both a passage of time and progress made on the stalled renovation.)

*(**RON** sits in a newer, nicer recliner. He drinks a beer. His face catches the glow of the old television as we hear from its speaker –)*

TV HOST. Today, the terrifying story of a metaphysical nightmare turned reality. Meet a recluse artist who paints in blood vivid depictions of his own interdimensional travels with hostile spirit beings he calls –

*(TV cuts abruptly to snow. A moment later, headlights through the kitchen window. A supposedly sober **RON** turns off the TV, pulls the remaining beers from the fridge, gathers the empties, and runs off to the bathroom.)*

(Three beeps.)

*(The toilet tank lid scraping, bottles clinking from off as **JOE** shuffles on with a walker, **RICKY** navigating. **RON** returns, closing the door behind him.)*

RICKY. What the fuck was that noise?

RON. Welcome home, father, brother.

RICKY. Did you break the toilet?

RON. It's kind of personal if that's okay, go use Dad's.

RICKY. Ron, where the hell have you been?

RON. Working, Ricky Lake.

RICKY. You haven't been here in two weeks.

RON. He was in the hospital!

RICKY. You didn't go to the hospital either.

> (**RON** *audibly burps.*)

Are you –

RON. She told me to move out, you fucking prick. That's what I are, am, okay? Now fuck off.

RICKY. You're talking about –

RON. Eva! Eva! / Eva!

RICKY. You cut me off! I was showing you I know now!

RON. Hey you know what, I don't want a fucking kid anyway, okay? Fuck that!

> (**RICKY** *breathes in to speak and –*)

And don't you fucking say you're sorry to me.

> (**JOE** *moans and tries to get up from the recliner.*)

RICKY. No, Dad, sit. Ron, look. Brand new, it's all tricked out.

RON. Yeah I already broke it in, give it here, I'm an expert.

RICKY. Okay but no massage, he's kind of brittle.

RON. Brittle is the ideal candidate, you wanna crunch all that shit up, watch.

(**RON** *pulls the recliner arm and the chair flops open,* **JOE** *flying back, grunting.*)

RICKY. Careful, my God!

RON. He's fine. Dad, I'm sending you out on mode *shiatsu*, turboboost engaged with a nice warm seat in 3, 2, 1, enjoy your ride.

> (**RON** *turns on the massager and we instantly blip to* **JOE**'s *perspective: the recliner at tremendous speeds through space.* **RICKY** *turns it off and we're back, normalcy.*)

RICKY. He doesn't like it.

RON. He loves it man, he's just misaligned.

RICKY. They said he's officially a fall risk.

RON. He's been falling since the eighties, he knows how to land.

RICKY. His balance got worse, he's all over the place.

RON. Yeah but he's clean right?

RICKY. There's no bar at the hospital.

RON. He's fucked, he's on something.

RICKY. Antibiotics for the staph infection, Ativan so he doesn't have a seizure, low dose, plus all his normal stuff.

> (*The notification sound of a well-known gay hook-up app.* **RICKY** *looks at his phone.* **RON** *looks over at* **RICKY**, **RICKY** *wonders if* **RON** *knew what that was.* **RON** *looks away, toward the bathroom door.*)

RON. Yo I can watch him if you got somewhere else to be.

RICKY. You're trying to get rid of me now?

RON. It's Friday night, we don't all have to sit here. I'm being nice.

> *(The app sounds another notification.*
> **RICKY** *checks his phone and sees a strange
> looking cock.* **RON** *gets the feeling of the cock's
> strangeness from the look on* **RICKY**'s *face.)*

RON. Oh my God, GO!

RICKY. Fine! But check his dressing for blood, he went
deep, it's still packed.

RON. Wait a minute, what the fuck did he do it for?

RICKY. He thought something was in there. Go brush
your teeth before Angie gets here okay, she's not stupid.

> *(***RON** *gets closer to* **RICKY**.*)

RON. Let me ask you something, Ricky. I've been putting
shit together.

RICKY. You're so fucking gross, get away.

RON. Think really hard, okay? So a very long time ago, up
on the roof with Dad –

RICKY. I don't care, Ron!

RON. Before the shingles it was all tile, we were up there
all the time.

RICKY. A few times.

RON. Way more than that and Angie couldn't come with
us, Mom said no.

RICKY. Stop talking about Mom.

RON. Hey you said her name first, you woke her up.

> *(Three beeps.)*

> *(***RON** *has scared himself now. They wait for
> Mona's ghost to enter, but it's just –)*

ANGELINA. *(From off.)* Why the fuck did they let him out
so late?!

RICKY. They just dump you on the curb with prescriptions.

(**ANGELINA** *enters.*)

ANGELINA. Did you see the social worker, did they give you places to check?

RICKY. Where the fuck were you? I don't like it here alone.

ANGELINA. *(Taking her note from fridge, pins it to* **RICKY.***)* At Crystal's, it was six days, you're fine, I sent you a Post-It.

RON. Let's talk business tomorrow, we should celebrate!

ANGELINA. He's dying, Ron, what do you wanna celebrate?

RON. He's not fucking dying, don't put that out there!

ANGELINA. Wernicke-Korsakoff Syndrome, was I right?

RICKY. Yeah and some other things, it's all connected.

ANGELINA. He needs B vitamins, that's what Crystal said, her dad was like this too.

RON. Everyone is fucking gay now.

RICKY. B vitamins but not orally, / he needs weekly injections.

RON. Orally haha, oh my God he has to go in for shots now?!

ANGELINA. What about dialysis?

RICKY. Hey let's talk when Ron isn't, I don't know, whatever.

ANGELINA. Why, what is Ron? Whatever what?

RON. Is he dying or not?

ANGELINA. *(Referring to her textbook.)* Wernicke's encephalopathy, Korsakoff's psychosis. Caused by extreme alcoholism and a lack of thiamine. Vocal aphasia, means he can't speak correctly, in his case not at all.

RICKY. The doctor said that won't change.

RON. Yeah but keep your fingers crossed.

ANGELINA. *(Still reading.)* Yep, he definitely sees imaginary shit.

RON. That's probably normal sometimes for some people.

ANGELINA. Hallucinations, dementia, psychosis. This is it. We're done. It's too big for us.

RON. So what exactly are you saying, are we putting Dad down?

(*Doorbell rings.*)

ANGELINA. Who is that?!

RON. Oh fuck yeah, I forgot! I ordered welcome home pizzas!

(**RON** *runs to get them.*)

ANGELINA. Don't order pizza if you don't live here!

RICKY. You sound real good saying that aphasia endaloppatheez shit.

ANGELINA. I know you're losing your mind here but you can't blame me.

(*Three beeps.*)

RICKY. It's just like here we are, in need of a fucking nurse.

ANGELINA. Are you seriously gonna play the asshole your entire life?

RICKY. There's a red eye to JFK.

ANGELINA. You better not, Ricky, / what is *wrong* with you?

RICKY. My head's getting sick over here, / I'm not helping him anymore.

ANGELINA. You messed your own head up, stop lying. Okay so help *me*!

(Pause.)

RICKY. What does he need?

ANGELINA. Are you asking my professional opinion?

RICKY. Sure.

ANGELINA. Full-time care.

> *(Voices of* **RON** *and* **DELIVERY DRIVER** *flirting.)*

Ron asked about the empty room upstairs, he might come back.

RICKY. What happened over there?

ANGELINA. Eva untied her tubes, they thought a baby would help their whole, I don't know, don't say anything but Ron can't and he won't go see why and she's all like –

> *(Front door slams.)*

RICKY. He tells you this?

ANGELINA. No, Eva does. I talk to her online.

> *(***RON*** *comes in with pizzas already eating a slice as* **ANGELINA** *leaves.* **ANGELINA** *slams her door.)*

RON. There's gotta be something they can do for him more than this.

RICKY. I'm open to suggestions.

RON. Hey you know that YouTube video where that guy is like completely bent in half? And then he gets entirely unbent by the end, like they crack his neck and then he's fine.

RICKY. So you think maybe a chiropractor for Dad?

RON. Throw his voice back into socket, ass to throat, everything's linked.

(Beat.)

RICKY. You smell like beer.

RON. Well that's weird, I'm not drinking any beer, you see any beer?

RICKY. You're such a freak, it's hard to tell if you're –

RON. If I'm what, motherfucker?! You call me a fucking freak one more time!

RICKY. You talk to Eva like that? Is that why she left you?

*(Beat that is **RON** stunned or feigning it, then –)*

RON. Eva didn't leave me you stupid, she's out with her friends.

*(Beat that is **RICKY** recognizing **RON** isn't well.)*

RICKY. Oh. Okay, good. Hey, you should relax. Watch some TV, we'll talk over coffee.

RON. Wait. Ricky. What if those kids up there on the roof were us?

RICKY. What kids?

RON. I don't know, I'm trying to see but I can't, like it slips out of the – you know what I mean? I think I need to retrace my steps.

RICKY. Why don't you turn on a movie or something?

RON. I'm trying to talk to you about something serious here, Ricky!

RICKY. No Ron, you're fucked up and you're gonna get yourself sick.

RON. I don't fucking care anymore, how about that?

RICKY. Okay good, then neither do I!

(RON lunges at RICKY, cornering him. It feels very dangerous.)

RON. Go to your fucking gay bar orgy!!! Open up every hole you got, see if I give a shit!! Get out of my fucking face!!!

(After a moment, RON lets RICKY go, returns to the television.)

(RICKY, terrified, grabs his car keys and begins to leave.)

So what's your poison these days, lemme guess. Looks like uh – what is it, cocaine?

(RON eats at RICKY for a moment.)

RICKY. Ron.

RON. What?

RICKY. Save me some pizza.

(RICKY leaves.)

(Three beeps.)

(Door slams. Car departs. RON goes to the bathroom, toilet tank scrapes, cracks open a beer, returns with it. JOE points to the ceiling again.)

RON. I'm trying but they won't go up there.

(RON drinks. A split-second, space-travel blip from JOE and the recliner.)

Two

(3:30 AM, early Saturday morning.)

(A strong moonlight off the pool shimmers against walls.)

(Three beeps.)

(A strange figure in shadow appears from the entrance hall, then stumbles desperately toward the fridge, ripping open the door. It is **RICKY***, disheveled and glowing in the light.)*

(He opens a pizza box and eats ravenously, wedging his body partially into the fridge's interiority.)

(The sliding glass doors to the pool suddenly sweep open. **RICKY** *freezes, seen.)*

RICKY. Who the fuck is it?

> *(**ANGELINA** coughing from outside. She enters, a puff of smoke preceding her.)*

ANGELINA. So you're going to gay bars without me now?

RICKY. Why's it smell like weed?

ANGELINA. Remember when you were too scared to go alone? You were terrified of AIDS.

RICKY. Because of that guy on *The Real World*. It freaked me out.

ANGELINA. So how do you go to a bar sober, what's your secret?

RICKY. I drank Diet Coke and played video poker.

ANGELINA. You left me a fucking mess.

RICKY. Ron was supposed to be watching him.

ANGELINA. Ron is currently walking to the Circle K for something a little bit harder.

RICKY. Oh no, he's drinking again?

ANGELINA. Fuck you.

RICKY. What, Angie?! He told me to go let off steam!

ANGELINA. He wanted you gone, you knew that.

RICKY. Yeah so I went, he's fucking crazy. Three different people at one time.

ANGELINA. Who does that remind you of?

RICKY. Ron is not Dad.

ANGELINA. He's really working on it.

RICKY. He loves that motherfucker.

ANGELINA. He's like addicted to Dad. Last time Eva left, he came over all the time.

RICKY. She'll come back.

ANGELINA. Ron needs Eva. He requires her. Eva made him these healthy salads.

RICKY. He was a machine.

ANGELINA. That whole ten years, best shape of his life, all Eva. / He was fucking ripped.

RICKY. Yeah he was ripped, I think the lesson here is don't give away half your renal system to a fucking monster.

ANGELINA. They're both going down, Ricky.

RICKY. No way. Ron is tough.

ANGELINA. No, Ron has to be kept, he falls apart by himself.

RICKY. Maybe that's his big lift here, he finally becomes self-sufficient.

ANGELINA. You didn't get fucked tonight, did you?

RICKY. Jesus Christ, no.

ANGELINA. Good. I'm sure your boyfriend Brian greatly appreciates your fidelity.

RICKY. I mean Brian really fucking better, I'm more attractive.

ANGELINA. Brian broke up with you. He said you're out of control.

RICKY. How the fuck do you know that?

ANGELINA. I asked him online.

RICKY. I don't want you talking to people I know online!

    (**ANGELINA** *receives a text.*)

Who the fuck is that, Brian?

ANGELINA. No. It's Crystal.

RICKY. Oh my God, are you in trouble with this woman?

ANGELINA. *(Excited.)* She might be able to take care of Dad during the day, one of her patients is close to dying!

RICKY. I can't do this right now.

ANGELINA. I checked and disability covers some which is cool since you're so fucking cheap.

RICKY. Hey does Ron bring burritos on Saturdays?

ANGELINA. I stayed up figuring this out when I said I wouldn't! I called people at home!

RICKY. *(Channeling a Spice Girl.)* Yes okay and I appreciate that but I wanna, I wanna, I wanna, I wanna, I really really really wanna eat a cold pizza. With my sister like we used to do when there was nothing else that we could do.

ANGELINA. You're so weak it's actually appalling.

RICKY. Okay fine if you're not gonna eat at least do me a favor?

ANGELINA. No more favors.

RICKY. Yes, here, hold a slice for show. So I don't feel like a pig?

> (**RICKY** *dangles a slice.* **ANGELINA** *unenthusiastically takes the piece. She holds it like a strange object. She pulls a pepperoni, sucks the oil.*)

It's those fucking munchies, right?

ANGELINA. Weed was never my problem. Hey you know Ron can't gain any weight, right?

RICKY. Cry me a river.

ANGELINA. He eats all day and nothing happens which blows my mind.

RICKY. He's gonna be okay.

> (**ANGELINA** *gets up, goes to the bathroom. Toilet tank lid scraping. She returns to the couch with the beer.*)

ANGELINA. Toilet tank. He's hiding them. But you already knew that.

RICKY. I was giving him the benefit of the doubt.

ANGELINA. Those are gonna kill him.

RICKY. Give me the beer.

ANGELINA. Where's my benefit of the, I'm feeling left out!

RICKY. Listen, you're stronger than us.

ANGELINA. Not saying much, you're both fucking pussies.

RICKY. Nice, Angelina, thanks a lot.

ANGELINA. I don't know why I said that.

(**RICKY** *suddenly recognizes the silk house gown* **ANGELINA** *is wearing.*)

RICKY. What the fuck are you wearing?!

ANGELINA. What?

RICKY. That...negligee?! What the fuck is that?!

(**ANGELINA** *looks down at the silk house gown she's had on, startled, having forgotten.*)

ANGELINA. It was on the hook in the bathroom.

RICKY. Why, who put it there?!

ANGELINA. Dad's been going through Mom's boxes at night.

RICKY. Dad or you?!

ANGELINA. What's your problem, Rick?

RICKY. It's like she's walking around, I don't like it.

(*Pause.*)

ANGELINA. Crystal reminds me of Mom.

RICKY. You barely knew Mom.

ANGELINA. Me and Mom used to go camping by ourselves.

RICKY. What?

ANGELINA. When her and Dad got too rough with each other, me and Mom left.

RICKY. Yeah you went over to Grandma's.

ANGELINA. No we went camping, I was there.

RICKY. When was that, weren't you only like –

ANGELINA. Five years old, she kept a tent in the van. We stopped for food and booze on the way.

RICKY. And you just now remembered this?

ANGELINA. *(Quite stoned now.)* Yeah, in my body. I mean I can't remember if I remembered before now but it's familiar so I must have. The whole world is like. Crystal says our dimension is sliding into another one and that's why everything fucking sucks.

> *(Here **ANGELINA** finally takes a large bite of pizza. **RICKY** notices, but does not stop her. He joins in, their pace picks up during the following.)*

Mm, I ate all the food in one night thinking we'd pack up the tent and leave the next day but then I just starved the rest of the time. Didn't do that again. Scariest part though, she'd get up in the dark, go outside screaming bloody murder in the middle of the night. Gone for hours or it felt like it.

RICKY. What did you do?

ANGELINA. I got drunk for the first time. When I was five, in that tent. It was rum and Tampico Punch. I wanted to go with her. I had to understand. I haven't been able to stop understanding ever since.

> *(**ANGELINA** tries twisting open the beer, fails.)*

You've gotta be fucking kidding me!

RICKY. I don't think those are twist top.

ANGELINA. Fuck, I can't even do this right. It tore my skin.

> *(**ANGELINA** rummages through a drawer.)*

RICKY. What are you doing?

ANGELINA. I was gonna drink this at the end of what I just said, it was gonna be so good.

RICKY. Yeah but you didn't so stop trying.

ANGELINA. Six months Ricky. Yeah I know it's not very long, I fuck up but for six months I almost exclusively consume what's good for my stupid fucking body and mind.

RICKY. I think you should give yourself a break.

ANGELINA. That's what I'm doing! I'm tired of watching everyone else fall off!

RICKY. I didn't fall off tonight.

ANGELINA. I can smell you, I saw you get out of the Uber.

RICKY. No. I've been fucked up for a while, it isn't new.

> (**ANGELINA** *finds a bottle opener, cracks open her beer.*)

ANGELINA. No shit. Also I'm really sorry to hear that.

> (**ANGELINA** *drinks her beer, waits, feels the warmth.*)

RICKY. Why the fuck did you do that?

ANGELINA. So we can actually talk about something.

RICKY. We *were* talking.

ANGELINA. No we weren't, see, look, it's already so much easier like this.

RICKY. Hey aren't big things about to happen for you?

ANGELINA. No way, I'll be dead before you know it.

RICKY. Don't say that.

ANGELINA. (*Running her fingers through her hair.*) Look at this? I'm way too young for my hair to fall out like this.

> (**ANGELINA** *hands over hairs.*)

RICKY. I don't know, this is only like five hairs.

ANGELINA. Yeah but it's five hairs every single time, / they keep falling out.

RICKY. So stop pulling out hairs to show people! / It's gross anyway.

ANGELINA. They'd still come out if I wasn't checking, something's not right. I can hear blood pumping, I hear like a whoosh, like it's fighting with something, then I hear these pop rocks, something's fucking popping all over the place, like inside my veins, like in my brain. Ricky, my heart stops when I sleep.

RICKY. I guarantee you that isn't true.

ANGELINA. I know that, I'm not insane, but it does. I wake up choking, it's pounding, it's angry, it's back from its break, my heart takes these heartbreaks. And then I see these, like, flashing, it's like I'm, what did Crystal say, astral. Oh shit, I can't be a nurse.

RICKY. You already are one, right? Go get paid for it.

ANGELINA. You could've paid me.

RICKY. I'm not the bank.

ANGELINA. Yeah the bank gives out free pens, so what is it? Are you broke or something, did you lose your job?

RICKY. Of course I'm not broke.

> (**RICKY** *leaves to retrieve a beer from the toilet tank as* **JOE** *passes through the hallway and toward the family room, undetected by the* **KIDS**. *But we notice.*)

ANGELINA. Then what's taking so long?! I need this. I need my fucking life back.

RICKY. Don't need me. I'm not a reliable person. He can go fuck himself.

> (**RICKY** *returns with a beer, opens it. Drinks.*)

RICKY. Leave this state and never come back, that was the plan.

ANGELINA. You got pretty close.

(They clink beers.)

RICKY. You think he, uh. Ever. Regrets, no not regret, you think he's –

ANGELINA. Sorry? For standing around while you got jumped by a bunch of mechanics? Yeah buddy, he's sorry. Is that what you need to hear?

*(**RICKY** lays his head on **ANGELINA**'s shoulder.)*

Hey, what if we just killed him?

*(**ANGELINA** and **RICKY** laugh.)*

(Three beeps.)

About fucking time, Ron! Hey, how much you wanna bet he got Crown Royal?

RICKY. Hey, Ron! Get in here, together we are captain relapse.

*(Door slams. **JOE** appears in the kitchen window, looking inside for a moment. **JOE** bends over, disappearing from view.)*

Ron?

*(A ladder goes up outside the kitchen window. **JOE**'s feet up the ladder as **RON** enters from Joe's room, half-asleep.)*

RON. Where's Dad?

RICKY. Whoa where'd you come from?!

ANGELINA. You're already here? When'd you get back?

RON. I never left, he was yelling, I laid down next to him and now he's gone.

ANGELINA. Is he in there?

RON. No stupid, that's what I said!

> *(A loud thump from above. They look toward the ceiling.)*

ANGELINA. Oh shit. He's on the roof.

> *(They leave in a rush, **RON** lagging behind.)*

> *(Three beeps.)*

> *(**RON** grabs hidden beers from under the futon and follows.)*

> *(Door slam.)*

Three

> *(Up on the roof, moments later. A hot breeze, monsoon clouds moving in. Already climbed up,* **JOE** *stands precariously near an edge.* **RICKY**'s *head appears from below the roof's eaves.)*

RICKY. Dad stay right where you are.

RON. *(From below.)* No sudden movements, don't freak him out.

ANGELINA. *(From below.)* Try to keep him away from the edge.

RICKY. I'm coming up there with you, okay? Just like old times.

RON. *(From below.)* See, you remember! Now get up on the top step!

RICKY. There's a warning sticker, you're not supposed to!

ANGELINA. *(From below.)* Push off the ladder and throw your left leg up and over, then roll.

> *(***RICKY*** *tries but fails, his head disappearing from view with a crash as his siblings laugh. A dog barks as* **ANGELINA** *climbs onto the roof, followed quickly by* **RON**, *then* **RICKY**.)*

RON. Hey Dad? I brought up some beers.

RICKY. What the fuck do you think you're doing?

RON. Relax I'm only using them for bait.

ANGELINA. Oh my God, I feel so fucked up.

RICKY. You got that newborn baby tolerance, enjoy it while it lasts.

RON. Why, what happened Angie? What the fuck did you do?!

ANGELINA. That didn't count downstairs!

RICKY. That's between you and your higher power.

ANGELINA. I don't do that God shit.

RON. Weren't you like six months in?

ANGELINA. I still am! Weed doesn't count, I had one beer, you cunt! Ron you're a fucking asshole bringing that up here. Enjoy your roof obsession, get a life or something someday, oh my God I have to get down, how do I do this thing, getting down is scary.

> (*In preparing to climb down,* **ANGELINA** *inadvertently kicks over the ladder. It falls with a crash. Another dog barks.* **RON** *cracks open a beer, hands it to* **RICKY**. *Then he opens another.*)

RON. Angelina, you want one?

ANGELINA. No way, I'm not like the rest of you fucking losers.

RON. Dang ride your buzz, you already did the damn thing.

ANGELINA. I'd need seven or eight more to find even the tip of enjoyment.

RON. Haha, you said tip. Hey, I'll go to the store and get more if you wanna do it right.

RICKY. What if we climbed down the pergola and put the ladder back up?

RON. That pergola won't hold you, it's hollow, there's carpenter ants.

ANGELINA. You think maybe I can jump from here? It's only thirteen feet.

RICKY. Don't you roll your ankle like every other day?

ANGELINA. No, not anymore!

RON. We could all jump in the pool, it's deep enough.

RICKY. Yeah but how do we get Dad to jump in with us?

ANGELINA. Right, because the deck sticks out like five or six feet.

RICKY. Which means he'd have to propel himself forward somehow.

RON. So what if he got a running start?

ANGELINA. He won't just up and run.

RON. He'll crack his skull if he hits the deck.

ANGELINA. Or break his neck.

RICKY. Or his arms or his legs or his ribs.

ANGELINA. Exactly. Which is why we have to push him off.

RICKY. Wow you're really ready to get the fuck out, aren't you?

ANGELINA. I think if one of you runs toward him full force.

RICKY. You can't do that, he's like full of sawdust.

ANGELINA. Ron are you good for this?

RON. Yeah totally you mean like sack him.

ANGELINA. Right! Just full on, boom.

RICKY. He's gonna vaporize!

RON. He'll be fine, he'll never see it coming.

ANGELINA. This way he clears the deck.

RICKY. You don't even know if he remembers how to swim! What if he panics?

ANGELINA. Dad plug your nose! Ron you're clear for take off.

RON. Oh fuck yeah! Hey, pretend that's Kurt Warner!

(**RON** *backs up to gain more runway and just as he leans forward to run,* **JOE** *plops to a seat on the shingles.*)

ANGELINA. You fucking hesitated!

RICKY. He clearly has his own opinions about being catapulted.

RON. At least he's on his ass now.

(**RON** *looks at them affectionately.*)

This is nice, would you look at us? Together again?

ANGELINA. We share the same DNA, it means nothing.

RON. You sure we've never been up here together, all of us?

ANGELINA. Mom wouldn't let me.

RICKY. He got crazy up here, that's why not.

RON. *(Searching for a memory.)* Wait! Whoa, you remember that light?

RICKY. What light?

RON. Shit I don't know, I lost it, let me think about it. He was fucking intense. He'd just get. Bigger. He'd get louder. We'd listen to him, like? Preach? He gave these speeches.

RICKY. It was Dad drunk on the roof, maybe something worse, like I don't know, how do schizophrenics act? See nobody knew about brains back then, that was the problem.

RON. He was way more than drunk. Yo, listen I know everyone thinks I'm losing my shit right now.

ANGELINA. You lost it a few months ago, Ron, I message with Eva.

RON. Don't talk to people I know online, Angelina!

RICKY. Yeah she did Brian, too.

ANGELINA. Ron the salads alone, you really need to call her.

RON. I'm not calling her!

ANGELINA. You can't sit around here again, it's not good for you.

RON. It's what I need, I'm at a really hard place in my process!

RICKY. What process?

RON. I don't know, man, all of it, it's in process.

ANGELINA. Lying about Eva, lying about Brian.

RICKY. I don't need people knowing I'm on my own!

RON. Nobody's fucking paying attention to you, Ricky!

ANGELINA. I am, I have to make sure he's not dead.

RON. I'm dead.

RICKY. Why the fuck would I be dead?

ANGELINA. There are so many reasons we could be dead!

(**RON** *stands, looking up at the sky.*)

RON. Wait shut up a minute. Look right there, is that it?

RICKY. Is that what?

ANGELINA. What are you pointing at?

RON. That yellow dot, Ricky remembers.

RICKY. Ricky does not.

ANGELINA. I can't see anything, I think I have retinopathy.

RON. Okay then fuck it, never mind! It's gone now anyway, you guys suck.

RICKY. Let us know if it comes back.

RON. *(Explaining something to himself.)* No because it's not a constant, yeah exactly right, that's what I said. Then comes that noise. No, I don't, but I get the feeling of it sometimes. Sorry, I'm just thinking here, it was um yellow, sometimes it blinks. Hey what am I even thinking of Ricky, do you know what I mean? What was that?

> *(A slight gust in the breeze. Copper wind chimes.* **JOE** *raises his hand to the sky.)*

There! He's pointing at it! Look! Wait, where'd it go?

ANGELINA. Do you smell the monsoon?

RON. I think he was getting us ready for something else.

RICKY. So retrace your steps man, dreams come true, you wanted up here.

ANGELINA. Wait, Ricky, you said you're having dreams again, which one? The one before Mom died?

RICKY. The one with the catastrophic explosion but somehow Dad survives.

ANGELINA. Me too, only it's the other way around and Mom survives.

RON. *(Reorienting himself, physically and psychically.)* Wait okay so how do you go back inside your head, let me think about this, so sometimes, right, we'd sit here just like this.

RICKY. Yeah and then he'd be stupid and eventually we'd all climb down.

RON. Yeah but it wasn't right, it felt like, I don't know. Like right now I'm a little scared talking about it and I don't remember why.

ANGELINA. I shouldn't smoke weed, I wanna be normal again.

RON. He's calling something.

ANGELINA. What is he calling, Ron?

RON. *(Remembering.)* Ricky! He told us he went to outer space!

RICKY. Oh yeah, all the time.

RON. What? You said you didn't remember anything!

RICKY. I thought you meant something important!

RON. That feels pretty fucking important!

ANGELINA. What did he say, he just said like *hey you guys I went to space*?

RON. No, not like that. What did he say, Ricky? He said –

> *(Starting here, **RON** tells a story by lip-synching pre-recorded lines voiced by **JOE**, affected to sound as if being channelled from the past. Also starting here, the sensorial world of the roof very gently veers toward the surreal via soundscape, stage magic, etc.)*

JOE. *(Voice-over.)* I know it sounds scary but I'm telling you the truth.

RON. That's impossible, he has not.

JOE. *(Voice-over.)* So many times Ricky, I'd tell you stories but you can't be trusted.

RICKY. He told this one all the time, he never finished, he always got distracted.

JOE. *(Voice-over.)* Hey! Look right up there, you see that yellow light?

RON. You have to search for a while but it shows up eventually.

JOE. *(Voice-over.)* It's blinking. Right there, Rick. Just a little prick like you, easy to lose.

ANGELINA. Do stars blink?

JOE. *(Voice-over.)* It's not a star, it's not a constant.

RON. It's not always there so you wonder if you're crazy, we're not crazy, it's right there!

JOE. *(Voice-over.)* It moves around, it never stays still, but it always comes when I call. That's the only place I find any peace.

RON. It's something about the light.

JOE. *(Voice-over.)* On that light in a small but comfortable room. It's how I get around, they let me use it as long as I keep it up and running. I keep adding hallways, your mother helps.

ANGELINA. He was fucking with you.

RICKY. Are we on the same page now, just a bunch of Budweiser stories?

RON. It was real to him. You could tell, that's why it freaked us out.

> *(The story **RON** weaves suddenly comes to vivid life as **JOE** himself begins to voice his own dialogue live, now facing us. The layers of surreality added thus far should remain and **JOE**'s voice should be affected as the prerecorded lines were.)*

JOE. Let me tell you something about me that you can't tell anyone else. They're not human. And neither am I. Not all the way through. But as far as everyone else knows I'm just a man fixing cars. I know how to hide it. If you want proof, fine, say the word. I'll rip off my skin, I'll shred it to bits. You want a mess, I'll rip it to ribbons.

> *(A car drives by and honks out three beeps like those from the front door, but they sound strange and alien.)*

JOE. Listen to me, remember this your entire life. They're gonna sneak into your goddamn bedroom late at night and take you way the fuck up north. They'll slip through your air vents, out through the closet, coming from light sockets, from inside the fridge, and you'll have nowhere to hide. But don't worry about that. Come on up and see us, it's only me and your mommy.

RON. Are you serious, is Mom gonna be there too?

JOE. She's only dead on Earth, of course she will be.

RICKY. No, she wasn't dead yet, this was before.

RON. Shit, I'm getting it mixed up, I know.

> (**RICKY**'s *phone alarm goes off and* **JOE** *reverts to his prior state. A sudden shift in the nightscape that makes us realize we weren't in a regular nightscape anymore, that something strange crept in without our knowing it.*)

What is that? Your reminder to be gay?

RICKY. I was gonna get up and go running at four in the morning so yeah kind of.

ANGELINA. Oh my God, it's four? I have to go to bed or I'm gonna die.

RICKY. *(Looking at phone.)* Hey hold on, shut up!! It's today.

ANGELINA. Yeah that's how that usually works.

RICKY. No. I mean, Mom. It's her birthday. She would've been like –

ANGELINA. Sixty-three.

> (*A wind gust, chimes, clouds are coming in, some leaves blow gently by.* **JOE** *reaches up toward the sky, again. They look.*)

RON. Wait, okay, hand up at the sky.

RICKY. We should call someone to help get him down.

ANGELINA. Hand up at the sky, that's what you said before, Ron, then what?

RON. Yeah and then like something happens. What was it?

> (**JOE** *suddenly starts groaning. It gets louder.*
> *A dog barks.*)

RICKY. Dad, chill out!

ANGELINA. I'm gonna go try the pergola.

> (**ANGELINA** *briefly vanishes to check.*)

RON. Hey Ricky listen I don't know if we're getting down from here, man.

RICKY. What? What's wrong with you? Jump in the pool, go bring us the ladder.

RON. Hey but we're ready, we're gonna be fine!

RICKY. What the fuck are you talking about?

RON. We've been up there before, right?!

RICKY. See man this is why I never come home, y'all fucking crazy.

> (**ANGELINA** *returns.*)

ANGELINA. The pergola is not an option, there's carpenter ants. Ron, jump!

> (*There's a flash from far above, a hollow pop*
> *that is actually an immense release of energy.*
> *They look up at it.*)

RON. What the hell was that?

RICKY. Oh shit. You guys. I think I remember.

*(An enormous explosive sound. A wave of neon yellow light illuminates them with a downward roaring wind. Debris flies. **JOE** begins to rise into the air as the **KIDS** move toward him, wide-eyed, lifting to their toes, too. Reaching, following their father.)*

End Act Two

ACT THREE

One

("[ ]" in dialogue indicates a very brief technical glitch. As if the program running this strange place occasionally buffers, causing light and sound disturbances.)

(The deafening roar of extreme speed. Then a sudden arrival. We're on the bridge of Joe's spaceship which has taken the form of the never-before-seen family room.)

(Burritos and bottles and foil balls and pizzas and a dead Christmas tree all seem ready to fly off on their own.)

(A couple of table lamps are present, unlit, but will be later. There's also a transluscent window revealing dark and gelatinous movements from space creatures beyond.)

(Throughout and with intention, we hear sounds we've heard before in this play, but now bizarre and distant and alien.)

*(**JOE**, **RICKY**, **RON**, and **ANGELINA** are scattered about on furniture pieces whose placement seem to defy the laws of physics. They lay as if discarded, trickles of blood*

*from their ears and eyes. Parts of their bodies
flutter and vibrate, vanish, then reappear.)*

*(**MONA** hangs high above them from a
motionless ceiling fan that is tilted from the
weight of her body. She's wearing the same
nightdress that **ANGELINA** does, still.)*

*(An intense yellow light passes slowly behind
the window with a fiery glow. An external
hiss and the sound of deep rumbling. The
room shakes for a moment but no one seems
concerned, or present at all for that matter,
except for **JOE**.)*

JOE. Alright everyone, hold tight. A very long way butbut
[ ] we're finally here. Are you with me? Please saysay
[ ] something if you are.

*(The **KIDS** moan as if trapped deep inside
their own bodies, then suddenly stop, voices
muting.)*

Bring the body and the mind will follow. Here, grab on
to this sound and pull yourselves up, you haven't heard
this one in [ ] black Ford Ranger so I'm sending it over
[ ] this one in centuries. Okay, all together now.

(Three space beeps.)

ALL (EXCEPT MONA). *(Rapidfire rap, like a machine gun,
no emotion.)*

YO HERE'S A LITTLE STORY OF A GIRL AND HER BIZCOCHO

AS SHE'S RUNNIN' THROUGH THESE STREETS WITH HER
TETITAS AND HER TOTO

AND SHE SAYS THAT SHE DON'T WANT IT SO I BACK UP
AND BELIEVE HER

THEN SHE FEELS A LITTLE LONELY SO SHE LOWERS
DOWN HER STANDARDS

AND SHE PULLS ME TO HER CLOSELY AND SHE WHISPERS
    TO ME GENTLY

SINGING SOFTLY IN MY EAR THINGS AS I TREMBLE
    LENTAMENTE FROM HER

CHA-CHA FOO-FOO PUCHA-POON

PUT A BABY IN HER BASKET LIKE A SPERMATA-ZOON

> *(The sound of* **MONA***'s noose creaking as she sways a little.)*

JOE. Mona say something, don't just hang there.

MONA. *(Rapped without emotion through a choked voice.)*
YO. YO. YO.
IMA CUT A BITCH UP, IMA BE THERE REAL SOON
I GOT THAT CHA-CHA FOO-FOO PUCHA-POON
TOO MANY BABIES IN MY BASKET FROM A SPERMATA-
    GOON
[ ]

> *(Voice normalizes as she says –)*

Here I come, I'm coming, and I'm here.

ALL KIDS. *(Still not looking.)* Mother. Mama. Mommy. Mom. Mona.

ANGELINA. Mindreader. [ ]

MONA. My babies, my children, my personal demons.

JOE. Good. That's better. Piece by piece.

RICKY. Steven Sondheim.

RON. Homosexual [ ] brother who I love.

MONA. My airway's completely clear. Now let the beat drop.

> *(The sound of a body falling, a rope snapping, stretching.)*

ALL KIDS. Dad. Dad.

JOE. Take it in, put it back inside your [ ] eternal process.

MONA. HEY, LOOK AT ME!

> *(They do. The ground falls out from under them. They suck their teeth from the inertia and look away from her.)*

> *(Three beeps.)*

JOE. Try again. Listen to this sound and tell me what you see.

> *(The sound of the body falling again.)*

RICKY & RON. The bottom of her nightdress. The chair tipped over.

ANGELINA. Go scream in your room and dance with Kurt Cobain.

ALL KIDS. Just because you're paranoid don't mean they're not after you.

RICKY & RON. Mom? Mom?

RICKY. Hung. Hung.

ANGELINA & RON. Hanged! Hanged!

RICKY. Out to dry. On a rack. Hanged from a tree. On a tree. Christmas lights.

> *([ ] as information returns to the **SIBLINGS**. Then the cheerful sounds of Christmas as the tree goes up in flames.)*

ANGELINA. Our mother hanged herself from the ceiling fan.

ALL KIDS. In the family room on Christmas Eve.

JOE. Perfect, now take a step through.

ALL KIDS. *(A bluely resonant moan that gets louder.)* Maaahhhhhhhh.

(They reach into their mouths and produce a glowing neon yellow Christmas light. An external hiss and another bright light passes by.)

JOE. Almost there now, one more year, that's all we need.

(A year passes. The room's ambiance switches to something more cozy as the practical lamps mentioned earlier suddenly snap on. The sounds of space and the galactic hum of the vessel.)

Goddamn that took much longer than expected, I am so sorry.

ANGELINA. It's fine, at least I have my legs now.

JOE. What do you need those for?

ANGELINA. I need to run around the room screaming.

MONA. Oh shit Joe there's no way she would, right? She couldn't.

ANGELINA. No because I'm nowhere near a panic. I feel absolutely nothing.

JOE. Okay good, there she is, get her a drink.

ANGELINA. You seem happy that I'm numb.

JOE. No because we also feel nothing, we don't feel happy at all.

ANGELINA. But you were dabbling in the celebratory it sounded like.

MONA. Emotion performed to make you more comfortable.

JOE. Mona show them how we connect with truth around here.

*(**MONA** clears her voice.)*

MONA. I wish I were able to feel glad at seeing you all again, but I can't, it won't come. I do however appreciate my inability to feel dread at your anticipated loss.

JOE. Angelina, go next if you understand.

ANGELINA. I feel a duty to mark as momentous this experience of arriving in outer space with my siblings, my diseased father, my deceased mother, rigid fucking vocabulary shit, but it feels ordinary while it should feel extra, ugh, language is detached from ego, ugh, no personality and emotion, no I'd fucking hate this if I could, words are stiff.

JOE. It's a programmed speech, it keeps us calm. But feel free to zhuzh.

RICKY. You guys, I'm so fucking frightened right now, oh my God.

JOE. No you can't be, you don't sound like you am.

RICKY. Yeah because I fucking aren't [ ] I wish I are. Damn it I can't move.

JOE. What I'm hearing is you'd be angry if you could be.

RON. So would I be, furious if I could be that, if I could feel anything at all.

ANGELINA. So angry if I could be, my rage could tear down these hallways.

> (*A split-second screaming hellscape, then it's gone.*)

MONA. Furious at who then? Go on, tell me. I'm just making conversation.

RICKY. At you I'd be furious.

ANGELINA. For killing my mother.

RON. At the old fucking man for killing himself slowly when he's all I ever had.

ANGELINA. At my tiny little brothers for leaving me alone without consideration or care.

RICKY. At these macho men right here for making my life a living hell.

RON. At Ricky for decimating my low self-esteem, whoa decimating decimating, yeah exactly, decimating! Acting like he was fucking better than me.

JOE. All of that said. No one is actually furious, please confirm?

ALL. *(Quietly, as if to self.)* Correct. No fury. No anger. None. Quia non dimittet te.

> *(A tone sounds. A sound of a deep hum dropping in.)*

JOE. Good. Neutral. It's holding up. I think we can start with the questions. Ask whatever you want. And then I'll tell you something and then we're done and then you'll never be able to speak to me again.

> *(No one says anything for a while. A hiss from outside.)*

RON. Is this a spaceship?

JOE. Well I mean it's a little more esoteric than that.

MONA. It belongs to God and death and cosmic intelligence.

ANGELINA. What are we here for?

JOE. I have some information to share which might make it easier when I'm gone.

RICKY. Have we been here before?

JOE. Thousands of times. We practiced. Separately. But I needed you all at once.

ANGELINA. Why don't I remember any of this?

JOE. Because you'd go into shock and shit your pants. No, you'd only experience inexplicable dreams of catastrophic explosions. That was us. That was this. Those were attempts. Panicked awakenings.

MONA. Enough about that. Ask me anything, I'm not here for my health.

RICKY. Did it hurt when your neck snapped?

MONA. The neck didn't snap. I suffocated while staring at the Sears family photo crooked on the wood-paneled wall. Oh God, please tell me someone straightened it out.

RON. What was wrong with you? What did it feel like?

MONA. I spent my days staring up at darkness from the bottom of an endless pit, that's what it felt like. The world was intolerable without putting something from the outside, inside. And. Unfortunately. Hold on tight. I hated being a mother.

> (*The sound of falling, inertia momentarily, then they land.*)

RICKY. You didn't hate being Angelina's mother.

JOE. Only questions, Ricardo.

RICKY. You didn't hate being Angelina's mother?

MONA. Angelina was *me*, you two were your father. There had to be sides or else we all would've died. But it's important you know that lady wasn't me. At least that's what I have to believe. If I were able to love you dearly I would have much preferred it. That sounds like a lovely experience. Now. Is that clear?

ALL KIDS. Crystal.

JOE. Anything else for me? I'd like to set it all straight.

> (**MONA** *places a finger on* **JOE**'s *forehead.*)

MONA. Why did you burn holes through your brain, Mr. Joe?

JOE. First to feel good, then to feel fine, then to feel less, then to feel nothing. Maybe a lack of courage. Say what you want about your mother but she was always the kind of woman that could take matters into her own hands.

MONA. And I always told your father he'd be better off dead.

JOE. But something I had that your mother didn't was hope.

RICKY. How?

RON. Hope for what?

ANGELINA. What could you possibly be hopeful for?

JOE. Hope that one day I might actually remember the day that came before. A hope that I might be a friend to my children rather than a burden.

ANGELINA. If you didn't want to be a burden then why were you? Why didn't you try?

JOE. I did try, I do. Every morning is the first day of our new life. The first fifteen minutes of each and every brand new day were spent being better than I was the day before. In the shower I'd cry, I'd say *help me help me help me help me help me help me don't drink don't drink don't drink don't drink don't drink help me help me don't drink don't drink.* I'd say that, in between dry heaves and streams of puke burning up my throat, I'd hold myself, wrap my arms around my own body, give myself the physical touch I longed for from lovers, family, from anyone who might rest a hand on my disgusting shoulder, tether me back to the planet even for a brief instant so I might feel human again. But who would touch me? No one and of course not. I knew what I was. I do try, Ricky. For the first fifteen minutes of every day.

(Another object strikes the window. Some mid-air objects fall to the floor. No one panics, they just continue.)

RON. When will this end?

JOE. Momentarily. Or in a few months. Depending what you mean.

ANGELINA. And we won't remember this happened?

JOE. You will experience sudden instances of familiarity, unexplained feelings of dissonance. A certain touch, the blink of a light, a discrepancy in memory between brothers. All will point you toward this moment, but no. You'll never remember.

RICKY. What was the purpose?

JOE. Good question.

MONA. We are here to implant something inside of you.

RON. Oh shit, what is it?!

MONA. An unconscious softening for us in your spirit that might grow over time. And not because we want you to remember us fondly. But because your hatred for us will eat you alive if you don't eventually let it go. This should help you do that.

JOE. It wasn't easy. All of this. But it was the least we could do.

(Space sounds.)

RICKY. Dad?

JOE. Yes.

RICKY. Are you sorry you did absolutely nothing when they [ ] [ ] [ ] at the shop. You did nothing, Dad, are you sorrysorry? [ ]

RON. Hey this is Ron here, Roger, [ ] Dad I can confirm that was pretty fucked up? Are you sorry?

(A boom, then the chortled sickness of an engine that sounds like it's running on digital diesel, a real old space model.)

JOE. Quickly, anything else?

RON. Will you die soon?

JOE. Not soon enough for your immediate schedules but it's on deck.

ANGELINA. Will we stay by your side until the end?

JOE. Not all of you, some of you will go.

ANGELINA. Me, I have to go Dad, you know that, right?

JOE. Yes, Angel.

MONA & ANGELINA. Angel. Angel. Angel.

RON. What about me? Do I stay by your side?

JOE. I wish you wouldn't Ron but you will and there is no changing that.

RON. Yeah but it could be fun, right? Bachelor pad, right? Dad?

(A huge crash.)

RICKY & ANGELINA. I've been having those dreams again.

ALL KIDS. What are the words we should say?

(Now sounds stack in abruptly, like cues that were playing but are suddenly unmuted.)

(Cicadas first.)

(Then pool water lapping. Then gate shut. Then dog bark.)

(Another crash.)

JOE. *(Voice coming from further away, like in a cockpit.)* Go! Now! Get the hell out of here! I'm going down with the – [ ]

RICKY. Catastrophic explosion.

JOE. *(Voice coming from further away.)* No, it's not a catastrophe, not for me, not anymore! I found a place I can go!

MONA. *(Her voice is still with the children.)* You'll all find peace in the end, in the ground. I did.

JOE. *(Voice coming from further away.)* Go live your lives in the meantime. Go! Tell them, Mona!

ANGELINA. Mommy, will you miss us?

MONA. Probably not but I'll sure fake it til I make it. Joe? Will you miss them?

JOE. *(Voice coming from further away.)* Of course I will. But I've always got you with me. Right here.

> (**JOE** *pounds his heart three times and it echoes and reverberates. The sound of another object hitting the walls, this time it penetrates. They are vaporized and vanish.)*

Two

(Two weeks later. Morning. The renovation looks as complete as it's going to get. Ricky's suitcase sits prominently.)

(A Roomba travels across the stage toward its landing dock.)

*(**JOE** shuffles in from his bedroom, dressed in his work clothes. He stares blankly at the crawling vacuum.)*

(The Roomba lands and beeps and puts itself to sleep.)

*(Three beeps. Door slam. **JOE** leaves as **RICKY** and **RON** enter with burritos in hand and sunglasses on.)*

RICKY. You have to act normal when you meet her, Ron.

RON. I'm always normal.

RICKY. She's Dad's nurse, not yours. Hey, are you sure you're okay with this?

RON. I have to be man. I gotta get better for him. No, it's good. I like it here, Rick.

RICKY. I'm concerned.

RON. Why? She cute? She got that cha-cha foo-foo pucha-poon?

RICKY. Don't be disgusting or she'll quit.

RON. You remember that song, right? Real old school.

RICKY. No idea what you're talking about.

RON. MC Deadhead. Pucha Poon, 1991. Look it up!

(Three beeps.)

CRYSTAL. *(From off.)* Beep beep beep, well Jesus Christ, that was cute! Oh my God, wood panel gives me the creeps, no offense or anything. Oh, that picture is crooked as all hell, it's gonna drive me crazy if I don't fix it.

(ANGELINA *and* **CRYSTAL** *appear.)*

ANGELINA. Leave it that way, it's fine. And here's the kitchen, my brother fixed it up.

CRYSTAL. Which brother, the asshole who never helps you?

(A moment where they all realize **RICKY** *is here and just heard that.)*

ANGELINA. He's starting to, we'll see if it lasts.

CRYSTAL. You wanna introduce us?

ANGELINA. Shit, sorry. That's Ron, he'll be around.

RON. I'm the heterosexual brother.

CRYSTAL. You got something against gay people?

RON. So, Crystal? How did you and Angelina. Meet?

RICKY. Ron, stop it. She'll be here during the day while you're at work.

RON. Hey Crystal you want in on the daily burrito run?

CRYSTAL. So where did she die? I have a very active imagination.

(Beat.)

ANGELINA. Back there, you already saw it. I didn't wanna say. In case she was listening.

CRYSTAL. And what was the illness, you said it was long?

ANGELINA. Um. Mental? Addiction, too.

ALL KIDS. Our mother –

> *(They stop. That was weird, the unison. After a moment –)*

ANGELINA. Our mother hung herself from the ceiling fan on Christmas Eve.

CRYSTAL. Oh. You never said suicide. I'm glad you did though. There's no shame. People have a hard time.

ANGELINA. Wait so you're not leaving?

CRYSTAL. Leaving? No way, this is bingo money.

ANGELINA. Ricky, she's the best in the biz. Dad will be fine, right Crys?

CRYSTAL. Everyone, listen to your new Aunt Crystal. You are amazing children to him even though he might not deserve any of it. You know that right? And I promise I'll take care of him like he were my very own Joe.

> *(For a brief blurry moment, **CRYSTAL**'s face is **MONA**'s face. The **KIDS** get weird about the familiarity and scatter, talking over each other.)*

RICKY. / Cool. Uh, his meds are right here –

ANGELINA. / I need to check my hair, I'll be right back.

RON. / What a weird fucking lady.

> *(**ANGELINA** exits.)*

RICKY. – a benzo, prednisone, sirolimus, cyclosporine to make sure his body doesn't fully reject his kidney. We're checking on dialysis.

RON. And it's the kidney I gave him. From my own womb, isn't that fucked up?

CRYSTAL. I'm sure intentions were good all around, just be happy with the time you've got left.

RON. Yeah. That's the right attitude! Yes, Crystal!

(**RON** *goes into Joe's bedroom.*)

(*Offstage, cheerful.*) Hey Dad you ready for work or what?

CRYSTAL. What's that mean is he ready for work?

RICKY. He gets himself cleaned up in the morning. Ron pretends to pick him up for his shift.

CRYSTAL. So Dad is still bathing himself, I like that. Oh and what about food?

RICKY. Yep. All set. Right here.

(**RICKY** *opens the fridge. Individual containers with meals. Some with blue labels, some with red.*)

CRYSTAL. Wow this is pretty nice, it looks so organized.

RICKY. A meal-prep place. They do a lot of sick old people. Blue is for Dad, red is for Ron. Ron needs nutrition, too, it's just easier. And you get this really good deal for two.

CRYSTAL. You did good, kid. Listen, I know how hard this is, believe me. My own father was. You know. It's hard.

(**CRYSTAL** *touches his shoulder.* **RICKY** *pulls away.*)

(**RON** *guides* **JOE** *out on his walker.* **JOE** *holds a water bottle in one hand.*)

RON. Dad's gonna call out sick again today if no one minds.

CRYSTAL. Hi Joe! It's me! I'm your new buddy Crystal!

RICKY. Dad, she'll hang out with you in the daytime, then you and Ron have dinner, watch TV and then he'll be here when you sleep.

CRYSTAL. Joe do you need anything right now sweetheart? I'm at your service.

(**JOE** *vomits a little, it runs down his shirt.*)

RON. Aw fuck man!

CRYSTAL. Just let him make a mess.

RON. No fucking way, he has to start the day with a clean shirt. I'll get him a new one.

(**RON** *leaves with* **JOE**.)

CRYSTAL. (*Calling after* **RON**.) Hey I can get that, that's what I'm here for!

(*A TV turns on in the bedroom.*)

RICKY. Just let Ron do the first part of the day, okay?

CRYSTAL. Hey your dad smelled like vodka.

RICKY. Yeah. We just decided to. Let him.

CRYSTAL. I don't know if I can get behind that.

RICKY. You don't have to get behind it, just be cool.

CRYSTAL. Where does he get it from? He's gonna walk if it's not there, they always do.

RICKY. He's got water bottles all over the place filled with it, he has no reason to leave.

(**RON** *returns from Joe's bedroom and opens a cupboard in the kitchen. Inside, several magnums of vodka alongside water bottles already filled with Joe's preferred beverage.* **RON** *takes a few water bottles, places one in the recliner, then takes the other with him.*)

Ron will keep him stocked.

(**RON** *returns to Joe's room.*)

RON. He's terminal, okay?

CRYSTAL. He should be somewhere that can keep him sober. I can get you some brochures.

RICKY. He was born in this house. It's compassionate. I don't have to explain myself.

CRYSTAL. Then I have to pass. I'm so sorry.

       (**CRYSTAL** *begins to leave.*)

RICKY. I can do an extra one-fifty a week under the table.

       (*She doesn't stop leaving.*)

Two hundred by CashApp.

CRYSTAL. Venmo.

RICKY. Fine.

CRYSTAL. But only because it's you, Ricky.

       (**ANGELINA** *returns with a box.*)

ANGELINA. Okay, I'm out.

RICKY. Hey thanks for stopping by, non-resident.

ANGELINA. I forgot some shit.

       (*A moment as* **CRYSTAL** *observes their tension, then realizes she's intruding.*)

CRYSTAL. Hey, you know what? I need the toilet, I'm about to pee everywhere.

       (**CRYSTAL** *goes into the bathroom.*)

ANGELINA. Don't be weird about this.

RICKY. Yeah I'm trying not to be but it is, it's weird.

ANGELINA. It's fine, stop it. So where next? You're headed home?

RICKY. No, not yet. I have to go do something first.

ANGELINA. Oh. Well that's good. I'm glad.

RICKY. I came here for you, Angelina. Not Dad.

ANGELINA. So you're doing rehab again, how long is the program?

RICKY. I'm starting with thirty days.

ANGELINA. What about work?

RICKY. Angie, come on.

ANGELINA. How much time off are you taking? I haven't seen you take a single call, nothing.

RICKY. There was a severance.

ANGELINA. How the fuck are we gonna do this?

RICKY. Me, I'm gonna do it, I'm fine for a while. It was generous, and I'm qualified, okay, market is good, I'll be gold if I can just get myself. Like. You know?

ANGELINA. Ricky.

RICKY. What?

ANGELINA. I have to go. Have a safe trip. Do the work. Get better.

RICKY. Yeah you too. Get better, stay better.

ANGELINA. Oh please, I had one beer, a few tokes, and a piece of pizza two weeks ago, I'm not like you. Ron?!

(**RON** *enters.*)

RON. You know, he's been drinking about three hundred fifty milliliters less a day, I think he's cutting back.

ANGELINA. Ron, let's go!

(**ANGELINA** *exits. Three beeps.*)

RON. Hey, Ricky, I got some news for you. I just wanted to say that I'm not homophobic about you anymore, okay? But just keep it to a simmer, that's all I ask.

RICKY. Fuck you, Ron. Bye.

> (**RON** *taps* **RICKY** *on the arm and leaves. Door shuts, truck goes.* **JOE** *emerges from the hallway. He and* **RICKY** *lock eyes. After a moment,* **CRYSTAL** *opens the bathroom door. She sees she's still not supposed to be here and closes the door slowly.*)

Hey I gotta go Dad. I'll visit soon. Ron's gonna be here after work, Angie sometimes. But me, I gotta go for now. So? You good man?

> (*Nothing.*)

Hey. I know you can't say it, but. I forgive you anyway. And I hope you forgive me, too. Okay? You motherfucker! ...I love you.

> (**JOE** *stands up a bit more when hearing this.* **JOE** *pounds his heart three times.* **RICKY** *grabs his* **FATHER**'s *cheeks and kisses his forehead. Then grabs his suitcase and leaves.*)
>
> (*Three beeps.*)
>
> (*Car drives off. Toilet flush.* **CRYSTAL** *returns.*)

CRYSTAL. He left already? He didn't get my Venmo.

> (**CRYSTAL** *puts something in the microwave for* **JOE** *and then pulls up a seat next to him. They make eye contact for a while.* **CRYSTAL** *becomes* **MONA**. *Then –*)

MONA. (*Putting her finger on his forehead.*) Why did you burn holes through your brain, Mr. Joe?

(The microwave beeps, the food is done. **MONA** *looks deep into* **JOE***'s eyes. Leans all the way in, face to face.)*

Joe? Is that you?

(A momentary blip of sound and projection indicating a slip into Joe's cosmic interiority. It takes us to silent blackness.)

End of Play

THE WET BRAIN FAMILY HISTORY

	1958	Joe is born.
	1960	Mona is born.
	1960–1974	The two grow up in Scottsdale blocks away from one another.
Joe, 17 Mona, 15	1975	They begin to date in high school.
Joe, 18 Mona, 16	1976	Joe graduates and immediately begins work at his father's auto body shop. He drinks nightly, heavily. Mona drinks cautiously along with him.
Joe, 19 Mona, 17	1977	Joe and Mona become pregnant with Ron. Respective families are furious so of course they marry. Mona, who dreamed of being a nurse or even a doctor, leaves high school one year before graduation. No one tries to stop her.
Joe, 20 Mona, 18	1978	Ron is born. Mona becomes depressed and begins to drink excessively along with Joe. Ron spends much of his first year being cared for by grandparents.
	1979–1982	Mona and Joe are at each other's throats, frequently drunk and still very much children themselves. Ron bounces between home and his grandparents' until Mona recovers to a point of being functional. Joe's drinking becomes violent on occasions. After a particularly bad beating, Mona wants a divorce. But family and church encourage patience, adherence to vows, and another child.
Joe, 25 Mona, 23 Ron, 5	1983	Ricky is born. Mona is depressed again, but worse this time. Joe believes she's faking it and tells her this in very painful ways. Mona has a psychotic break at Christmas and is evaluated, treated, and put on medication. She stops drinking and the meds eventually bring tolerable numbness. Without her at his side, Joe begins to hide his booze and consumes in secret.

Joe, 26 Mona, 24 Ron, 6 Ricky, 1	1984	Eventually Mona feels so much better that she replaces her medication with nightly cocktails instead, or often mixes the two. Joe returns from his closet-nips and switches back to open excess. And as Christmas approaches, the pair descend into a violent blur of physical aggression and confusing sexual encounters that feel at once voluntary, but also repulsive and punitive. Mona becomes unintentionally pregnant.
Joe, 27 Mona, 25 Ron, 7 Ricky, 2	1985	Angelina is born. And for the first six months of the baby's life, Mona is miraculously changed, the depression lifted. She is present and bonds with Angelina in a way that she couldn't with the first two. Angelina won't remember this bonding, but her body and soul will. Ron doesn't recognize the warmth he's seeing expressed by his mother toward this new sibling. A depression returns to Mona around month seven, and, portpartum or not, it is the end of Mona's mental health remission. The bottom drops out completely.
	1986– 1989	All vices and mental incapacities afflicting mother and father progress during this time. Ricky and Ron stay with cousins and grandparents often, as they always have, but Angelina is kept at Mona's side. The boys are further distanced from Mona, seeing her choose Angelina over them, and form a brotherly bond that mimics the violence (and love) they see around them.
Joe, 32 Mona, 30 Ron, 12 Ricky, 7 Angelina, 5	1990	Mona and Joe fight. Violence becomes more frequent, cops are called. Mona flees extreme conflicts with Angelina in tow, taking her camping, leaving the boys behind. To her, Joe/Ricky/Ron are cut from the same monster man-cloth. It is here, too, that Ron and Ricky begin visiting the roof with Dad.
Joe, 33 Mona, 31 Ron, 13 Ricky, 8 Angelina, 6	1991	Joe has a violent incident in Wal-Mart and is hospitalized, diagnosed as bipolar, and put on medication that he refuses to take. Mona goes to bed one day and she stays there for months, getting up only to feed the children, smoke a

cigarette by the pool, or have another drink. She tells them: Mommy is sad so fuck off and go eat something. So Angelina and Ricky do. They eat as much as they can.

Joe, 34 Mona, 32 Ron, 14 Ricky, 9 Angelina, 7	1992	On Christmas Eve, Joe takes the children to their grandparents' for presents. Mona refuses to come and insists on staying behind. She hangs herself from the ceiling fan in the family room. Ron is the first to find her upon returning, followed by Ricky who sees less, just the blur of her nightdress. Angelina sees her swinging foot. Ron sequesters them in his bedroom and turns on Nirvana. Joe drinks a fifth of vodka and calls 911.
	1993– 2000	Family grief and a desolate stretch of time marked by the feeling that they are all suddenly closer but simultaneously moving irreconcilably away from one another at great speeds. They understand each other more now, but lack a language for love and care, so they find a language of ridicule instead. Ron graduates from high school and immediately starts working at the shop with Dad.
Joe, 42 Ron, 22 Ricky, 18 Angelina, 16	2001	Rehab One for Joe, court-ordered after a DUI. Ricky graduates high school and begins an accelerated BS+MBA program at Arizona State, living at home while working at the shop part-time doing the books. There he faces overt homophobic bullying that Joe does nothing about even when Ricky is beat within an inch of his life after a hookup-gone-bad with a down-low mechanic who just got scared. Ron still lives at home. Angelina is struggling to finish high school, not because of lack of intelligence, but because of circumstance.
Joe, 43 Ron, 23 Ricky, 19 Angelina, 17	2002	A year with less alcohol for Joe because he has to blow into a tube to get his truck to start. So he smokes plenty of weed to fill the gap. Ricky quits the shop and takes a job at The Phoenix Zoo as a tour guide. Joe is furious. Here something breaks even more between them but neither notices because everything is so broken already.

Joe, 44 Ron, 24 Ricky, 20 Angelina, 18	2003	Joe begins drinking exclusively again, and more heavily. On the few occasions when he can't time his drinking along with his transportation needs, Joe pays Ron to blow into the truck on Joe's behalf. Angelina finds out she can't graduate with her friends, takes summer school to make up a class she failed, and receives her diploma in the mail.
	2004–2005	Joe's parents, the grandparents that helped raise Ricky and Ron, die in a car crash. Grief again for the siblings, but hardly. When did they stop being able to feel? Joe is rid of the man he hated the most, inherits a business, and loses a mother in one instant.
Joe, 47 Ron, 27 Ricky, 23 Angelina, 21	2006	Ricky graduates from college and leaves for New York City, taking a job in the CFO's office of a small startup owned by a guy he fucked after Phoenix Pride. Angelina is devastated to lose her brother just as she meets the grown-up version of him. They just spent the summer gay-barring together and feeling close for once. Ron meets Eva and gets swept up in her healthy lifestyle. He hardly drinks anymore, eats these healthy salads, juices and stuff. He's ripped, in the best shape of his life and moves in with Eva, leaving Angelina alone with Joe.
	2007–2008	Angelina has worked retail since she was fourteen, works it now. In this house you didn't eat unless you had your own money. She tries going back to school a few times but life gets in the way. Meanwhile, as a young, virile, and highly-functional cocaine addict, Ricky is quickly promoted to VP of Finance. He's out every night, sleeping very little, and losing himself. Kid in candy shop, too much candy, candy make crotch itch.
Joe, 50 Ron, 30 Ricky, 26 Angelina, 24	2009	Rehab Two for Joe after doctors warn of rapid kidney decline. A healthy Ron begins smoking weed and Eva allows it, but only if he keeps up with his diet and workouts and doesn't become a slob. Eva joins sometimes. She doesn't realize that, for Ron, weed really is a gateway back to booze. But she'll soon find out.

	2010– 2014	A frightened Joe swears off booze, goes back to weed. But his kidney disease worsens, still. Angelina has more time on her hands now that Joe is a pothead and stays still. She goes back to the same gay bars she visited with Ricky. She wonders if there's a gay bar for women. She wants to know more women. Ricky goes to rehab and tells no one but work. He comes back strong, then relapses and slips back into an ever-worsening routine. Weed got boring so Ron has some beers now and then. Eva notices, she doesn't like it. They find out Ron can't have kids. Eva says it's okay with her but it's really not. Joe is drinking and smoking in equal measure. His lower back hurts on both sides.
Joe, 56 Ron, 36 Ricky, 32 Angelina, 30	2015	Joe is in renal failure and needs a new kidney. 6–18 months of sobriety is required for transplant list but he doesn't have that long. The kids test and Ron is a match. Angelina tells him don't do it, tells him Joe will ruin every kidney you give him, but Ron goes through with the surgery anyway, saving Joe's life, a life which most likely should have ended right there. Ron demands a pact of sobriety from his father and siblings. They loosely agree.
Joe, 57 Ron, 39 Ricky, 33 Angelina, 31	2016	Ron begins having health problems associated with losing a kidney. He insists he has been sober but no one knows for sure. He hasn't been. Angelina begins to smell alcohol on Joe and can't figure out how to tell Ron that his kidney is being abused. Ricky begins dating a man named Brian. Brian hits Ricky, but Ricky stays. And together they drink and get worse. Ricky tells no one. He never tells anyone anything. Angelina finds a journal from Mona's teenage years. Only a handful of entries, she didn't stick with it. But one entry professes a desire to become a nurse. Or maybe even a doctor. Angelina takes this to heart.

Joe, 58 Ron, 40 Ricky, 34 Angelina, 32	2017	Joe is arrested for a second DUI and begins having intermittent difficulty speaking. Angelina sounds the alarm and Ricky gets Joe in a rehab for the third time. Joe leaves rehab early and picks up where he left off. Ron is furious and begins to drink openly, excessively. He loses control and Eva makes him move out. For many months Ron sleeps on the futon at Dad's where together they drink heavily, kidneys be damned. Until Eva invites Ron back.
	2018– 2022	Angelina develops an affinity for cheap white wine from the gas station. Her binges and dark periods are usually limited to spurts of sudden income, like a tax refund, but the cheap wine she can afford. She eats more when she's drunk, bingeing in an old familiar way, and begins to gain a significant amount of weight in her isolation. She sends Ricky copious amounts of emails begging for help on multiple fronts. He ignores them because he is also ill himself. Ricky loses a promotion due to poor performance, puts himself through another rehab, and breaks up with an abusive Brian. He starts over. Joe's license is permanently revoked, Ron starts picking Dad up for work. Ron is on and off with Eva, their troubles tracking along the contours of Ron's sobriety, or lack thereof. Ron is often on the futon. Unable to secure his own alcohol, Joe begins walking to the store at night. His disease progresses, his voice becomes increasingly shaky until suddenly he stops making sense.

Joe, 64	2023
Ron, 44	
Ricky, 40	
Angelina, 38	

Ricky has relapsed again, his sobriety only lasting a few months, and is finally let go from his job. He has a night with Brian and hates himself for it. He begins having ominous dreams of home, the family room, people glued to ceilings. He wakes up terrified, overflowing with guilt and shame. He's depressed and sick. Then the email comes that says Angelina is leaving on the first. That Joe will have to take care of himself. Broken and losing it, Ricky decides he needs to be miserable in Arizona and not miserable in New York, at least for now. So he does the thing he's most afraid of: going home. Ron is about to lose Eva. Again. His health continues to decline and he does very little to change that. Joe becomes the only thing in Ron's life and Ron begins fully transforming into his father. Angelina is on her way out and has been visiting with the past, her mother's memory, projecting ideas of their forgotten relationship onto a new friend named Crystal. Joe is silent, busy building hallways no one else can see, preparing a place for them all to say goodbye.